Cowpokes
and
Desperadoes

Gary Paulsen

Cowpokes and Desperadoes

A YEARLING BOOK

Published by
Dell Publishing
a division of
Bantam Doubleday Dell Publishing Group, Inc.
1540 Broadway
New York, New York 10036

The trademark Yearling® is registered in the U.S. Patent and Trademark Office.

The trademark Dell® is registered in the U.S. Patent and Trademark Office.

ISBN: 0-440-40902-0

Printed in the United States of America

January 1994

10 9 8 7 6 5 4 3

OPM

Cowpokes
and
Desperadoes

Chapter · 1

Duncan—Dunc—Culpepper sat on the corner of the window watching his lifetime best friend, Amos Binder, pack his suitcase. Amos had a system. If it was semiclean and fell into the category of clothing—throw it in.

Dunc glanced around Amos's room. It looked as if it had been through a recent nuclear blast. Junk was thrown (Amos said it was strategically placed) everywhere. Dunc picked up a torn poster of a race car. Underneath was a rotten banana peel, a moldy sock, and a pair of jeans.

Amos grabbed the jeans and threw them into his suitcase. "That ought to be enough stuff for two weeks. This is so great! I've al-

1

ways wondered what it would be like to be a real cowboy. Can't you just see me riding the range, roping cows, and singing songs on the lone prairie? I'm lucky your uncle invited me to come with you."

"Uncle Woody said he was glad to have you. He's a little shorthanded at the ranch right now. Some of his hands just recently quit."

Amos sighed. "Melissa is going to be so impressed."

Melissa Hansen was the girl Amos dreamed about—the only girl in the world, as far as Amos was concerned. He spent most of his life working on schemes to get her to notice him. Like the time he joined the circus as a trapeze artist and ended up landing on her and breaking her arm. But not even that did it. So far nothing had worked. But Amos never gave up hope.

"This cowboy thing could turn out to be a lot more work than you think," Dunc said.

Amos's eyebrows went up. "Work? I thought all cowboys did was ride around and look at cows."

"I don't want to discourage you, but there's

a lot more to it than that. The horses have to be fed, and the barn has to be—"

Amos put his hand up. "Don't be so negative. This trip is going to be fantastic. Besides, I think it'll be good for me to get away for a while. Kind of let things settle. Due to the fire and all."

"Fire?"

"Yeah. Our kitchen caught fire last night. It really wasn't that big a deal—mostly smoke. The fire department put it out in no time."

"How did it happen?"

"I was watching my cousin, little Brucie, in the back yard. You remember little Brucie?"

Dunc nodded. "Cute kid. Last time he was at your house, he ate your goldfish."

"That's him. I had baby-sitting duty while my dad was cooking hamburgers on the grill. That's when the phone rang. I was pretty sure it was Melissa calling to talk about my trip to the ranch and how impressed she was about my being a cowboy."

Dunc nodded again. He knew it couldn't have been Melissa. It was never Melissa. Had never been Melissa. Would never be Melissa.

3

"She likes for me to get it on that all-important first ring, so naturally I took the shortest route possible to the phone. There was just one problem—the barbecue grill was in the way."

"You knocked over your dad's barbecue grill?"

"No. You would have been proud of me, Dunc. I was in classic form, with just the right amount of momentum. My stride was great— I hurdled it. I wish someone could have taken my picture. I was incredible."

Dunc frowned. "If you didn't knock over the grill, then how did you start a fire?"

"I had almost cleared the grill when things sort of went downhill. A flame shot up and my pant leg caught on fire. I think I could have handled it and still made it to the phone if it hadn't been for the marbles."

Dunc shook his head. "You lost me."

"Little Brucie. He left his marbles on the kitchen floor. I'm pretty sure he did it on purpose. He's only three, but he can be vicious. Anyway, I hit them at a dead run, lost my balance, and slid under the table right into the trash can. It was full of paper. My pant leg ignited the paper, and that's how the fire started."

"Did you get to the phone?"

"No. Amy answered it. She claimed it was someone selling tickets to the firemen's ball. My dad bought quite a few."

Dunc tried to keep from smiling. "I can see why it might be better for you to go out of town for a while."

"Yeah, I hope it'll give my parents time to calm down. I think they will, unless they listen to my sister. Amy says this is her big chance. She's going to try to talk them into moving to another part of the country while I'm gone."

"Don't worry, Amos. She's probably kidding."

"I don't know. You should have seen the gleam in my dad's eye when she first suggested it."

Chapter · 2

Amos arrived at Dunc's house the next morning right on schedule. He was wearing a black cowboy hat that kept slipping down over his ears, boots that would have fit Ronald McDonald, and a belt buckle the size of Montana.

Dunc scratched his head. "That's quite an outfit."

"Thanks. I borrowed it from Ernie Weller. His older brother used to work for Cowboy Bob's Pizza Palace. I didn't want to show up at your uncle Woody's ranch looking like a dude."

Dunc picked up Amos's suitcase and headed for the car. "You look like a real cowboy, all right. I think it's the gold pepperoni pizza on the front of the buckle that does it."

At the airport, Mrs. Culpepper insisted on pinning name tags on them and kissing Dunc good-bye right out in public where everyone could see. She started for Amos, but he ducked under her arm and headed for the plane.

A flight attendant named Cindy showed them to their seats. Amos took the one by the window.

"Parents are so weird," Dunc said. "They let us go all over town by ourselves doing whatever we want. But when we are confined in an airplane, thousands of miles in the air, with no possible means of escape—suddenly they get all mushy and worried and pin a name tag on a guy, like he was some kind of a baby."

Amos leaned back in his chair. "Who can figure parents?"

Cindy came by to make sure they were comfortable and find out if they wanted anything.

Amos ordered a soda, peanuts, and a pillow. "That Cindy sure is nice. I bet Melissa will be a lot like her when she grows up."

Dunc yawned and closed his eyes. "My mom probably bribed her to keep an eye on us. I'm going to take a nap. Wake me when we get to New Mexico."

Amos looked around the plane. No cowboys. Real cowboys probably don't ride in airplanes, he thought. He would have asked to be sure, but Dunc was already snoring.

Amos took his hat off and loosened his buckle. Another thing he needed to find out was how cowboys sit down wearing these big buckles and breathe at the same time.

He picked up a magazine and thumbed through it. Directly behind him he could hear two male voices talking in low tones.

". . . it shouldn't be hard. We've got him right where we want him. Everything's all arranged. That Culpepper character will soon be history."

Amos sat up. Culpepper? History? He grabbed Dunc's arm and started shaking.

Dunc's eyes flew open. "What?"

Amos put his finger to his lips. "Shh! Listen."

The voices continued. "Culpepper's an old

9

man. He hardly has any real hands left who'll work." The speaker laughed sharply. "We've managed to convince them all to leave."

"Amos," Dunc whispered urgently, "we have to go to the bathroom."

"We do? I don't think so. I mean, maybe you do, but I don't—"

"Come on." Dunc pulled him down the aisle.

There was barely enough room for both of them to stand inside the tiny rest room. Dunc locked the door. "Amos, what did you hear before you woke me up?"

"Not much. They just said everything was arranged and Culpepper would be history. For a minute there, I thought they were talking about you. I guess it must have been somebody else."

"Don't you get it? Those guys weren't talking about me. They were talking about my uncle Woody—Woody Culpepper."

"Why would anybody want to hurt your uncle? I thought you said he was a nice guy."

"He is. I can't figure why anyone would be after him. Hmm."

Amos closed his eyes. "Oh, no. Don't. Please don't start with that."

"What?"

"That sound. Every time you make that sound, I wind up in trouble. This is supposed to be a nice, quiet, fun vacation. No mysteries. Why can't we do it that way just once?"

"Amos, my uncle could be in some kind of trouble. We can't just pretend we didn't hear anything."

"I could try. My uncle Alfred—the one who picks his feet?—anyway, he's always saying things my mom tells me to pretend I didn't hear. Like the time he dropped his cigar in his lap and burned a hole through his pant leg, and—"

Dunc interrupted. "This is different. These guys sound serious."

Amos sighed. "I suppose you have a plan?"

"The first thing we need to do is ID those two guys behind us."

"Are you going to talk like a secret agent for the whole vacation?"

Dunc opened the bathroom door a crack and peeked out. "Wait a few minutes, then follow me back to our seats. We don't want to be noticed, so try to act nonchalant."

"What does that mean?"

"Natural. Try to act natural."

He shouldn't have said it. They argued about it later. *Natural* for some people means one thing, but for Amos, it takes on a whole new definition.

Dunc was halfway to his seat when he heard the crash. Amos tripped coming out of the rest room. He did a nose dive into the flight attendant's serving cart. Several people who were unlucky enough to have aisle seats were drenched with ice water. One man was screaming. He thought he had been shot until he discovered it was only tomato juice on his shirt.

When Dunc finally found him, Amos was stuck under the seat of an irate lady passenger. She had a grapefruit on her head and was grinding her high heel into the middle of his back.

It took some doing, but Dunc finally managed to convince the woman that Amos was harmless. She let him up but made him promise not to get out of his seat again until the plane landed.

"So much for not drawing attention to ourselves," Dunc said.

He led Amos back down the aisle to their seats. Before they sat down, Dunc casually leaned around the back of his seat to get a look at the men in the row behind them.

Empty.

Not one person was sitting in the whole row.

Now, why would they have moved? Dunc thought. They couldn't have known . . . or could they? He looked down at the name tag on his shirt. His last name was in bold print.

Culpepper.

Chapter·3

Uncle Woody met them at the airport. He was a tall, lean man with a twinkle in his brown eyes. He gave Dunc a bear hug and shook Amos's hand as if he were pumping water. They loaded their bags into the back of his ancient pickup truck and headed for the ranch.

Dunc answered all the usual questions about his family. Then came the question he was waiting for.

"Did you boys have a good flight out?"

"It was a pretty smooth flight, but we did have something strange happen. Two men sitting behind us were talking about taking care of someone named Culpepper who owned a ranch." Dunc looked over at his uncle.

The tall man rubbed his temple. When he spoke, he chose his words carefully. "It couldn't have been anything important," he said. "You probably had the misfortune of sitting in front of our distinguished bank president, J. B. Grimes. He and I have had some unpleasant dealings lately. He makes a lot of threats, but he's mostly full of hot air. Don't let it bother you."

"Oh, we won't." Amos glared at Dunc. "Will we?"

Dunc ignored him. "You mentioned in your letter that a lot of your hands had quit. Did they tell you why?"

"They all had their reasons, I guess." Uncle Woody shifted in his seat. "It's really lucky for me that you boys came out when you did. I can sure use your help until the new hands get here."

"We're the lucky ones," Amos said. "Riding, roping, herding them little dogies . . ."

"Now, hold on, pardner." Uncle Woody grinned. "We do have a couple horses picked out for you boys, but you'll need to take it real slow. For the first few days, I'll have Juan show you around. Then if you're still willing, we'll talk about your chores."

"How much farther is it to the ranch?" Amos asked.

"Son, we've been on it ever since we turned off the highway. The Rocking C covers a good chunk of land. We'll reach the main house in about fifteen minutes."

Amos sat back and looked at the desert landscape. In the distance were rolling hills, and farther away, blue-gray mountains.

Uncle Woody slowed down. He was looking at some cows milling around a dirt tank. A cowboy was riding among them. When he spotted the truck, the cowboy turned his horse and took off at a dead run.

"What was that all about?" Dunc asked.

Uncle Woody pulled up beside the tank. "Another unwelcome visitor. We've been having our share of those lately."

He stepped out of the truck and looked around. The cows were gentle, and when they saw the truck, they headed for it and started bawling for food. Uncle Woody reached in the back for a can of grain and poured it into a trough.

Dunc slipped out the other side of the truck. "That guy doesn't work for you?"

"Nope. I'm not sure who he works for, but I think he was after these cows. If we hadn't come up on him, he might have pulled it off."

Amos walked over. "Are you serious? Cattle rustlers? I thought that stuff only happened in the movies."

Uncle Woody bent down to look at the track the horse had left. "Believe it or not, cows are worth a lot of money. We've had quite a few stolen lately."

"Have you called the police?" Dunc asked.

"I had the sheriff out here the other day. But so far he hasn't come up with anything." Uncle Woody straightened up. "Well, we'd better get a move on, boys, or Juan and Maria will be wondering what's keeping us."

"Do Juan and Maria work for you?" Amos asked.

"It's more like they work *with* me. Maria is Juan's grandmother. She's lived on this ranch almost as long as I have. Juan is my top hand, and Maria sort of runs the place. I couldn't make it without them."

Amos stepped in a pile of cow manure on his way back to the truck. He kicked hard in an effort to whip the slimy stuff off, but instead his boot went sailing through the air.

Dunc went on talking as if nothing unusual were happening. "How many cowboys do you have working for you altogether?"

Amos hopped around on one foot trying to get to his loose boot.

"Counting Juan, two."

Dunc opened the truck door. "You run this big place with two ranch hands?"

"Well, I work, too, of course. And you boys are fixing to help out. So now we have five."

Amos's hat slipped down over his eyes, and he couldn't see where he was going. He reached down for the boot, but his buckle wouldn't let him bend over. He wobbled, tried to regain his balance, and fell backward, seat-first, into another pile of cow manure.

Dunc sighed and closed the truck door. He walked over, helped Amos to his feet, and handed him his boot.

Uncle Woody laughed. "Amos, now you not only look like a cowboy, you smell like one too."

Chapter · 4

The pickup came to a stop in front of a white adobe ranch house. Tall cottonwood trees covered the front of it. A black and white border collie jumped the fence and ran to greet them.

"Boys, this is Suzy. I should have included her when I was naming our hands. She's a good one. Say howdy, girl."

The dog sat back and lifted one paw up and down as if she were waving.

The front door burst open, and a Mexican-American woman came bustling out of the house.

"Señor Culpepper, I am so glad you are back. The calls—they started again, almost as soon as you left."

"Now, calm down, Maria. You're going to excite the boys. I want you to meet my great-nephew Dunc Culpepper and his friend Amos Binder."

"*Hola,* boys. We are so glad you have come. Juan and I have been watching for you. Please come in the house. I have prepared refreshments."

Uncle Woody looked around. "Where's Juan?"

Maria pointed toward the barn. "Feeding the horses."

"That's supposed to be Billy Ray's job."

"Billy Ray left earlier. He didn't say where he was going or when he'd be back."

"Maria, take the boys in and show them to their room. I'll go find Juan and be right back."

Dunc and Amos followed Maria inside and up a carved wooden staircase. Their room had a set of bunk beds with a wagon wheel on the end, a double dresser, and a small leather couch. On the walls were pictures of horses.

Amos threw his suitcase on the top bunk and plopped onto the couch. "Isn't this ranch fantastic? It's just like I had it pictured! Maybe even better."

Dunc closed the door. "Amos, something strange is going on here. Haven't you been listening?"

"Yeah. I heard your uncle tell us it wasn't important and that we shouldn't worry about it."

"What about the phone calls and the cattle rustling?"

Amos shrugged. "This is New Mexico. Those things happen. The sheriff is working on it. Lighten up. Let's go downstairs and find those refreshments."

Dunc took a small pad of paper out of his bag and started making notes.

"Only you," Amos said, "would bring a notebook on a trip like this."

"I don't want to forget anything when we start to work on the case."

"Case? There is no case. Why do you have to play private eye everywhere we go?"

"Two men talk about my uncle being history, and then they disappear. Add that to cattle rustling and strange phone calls. I'd call that a case."

Amos stood up. "I'd call it time to eat. Are you coming?"

Dunc made a couple of quick notes and put his notebook away. "Right behind you."

In the kitchen, Maria was setting the table with all kinds of goodies. Amos had trouble figuring out where to start. He'd just stuffed a jelly doughnut into his mouth when Uncle Woody stepped in.

"Boys, I'd like you to meet Juan, my top hand."

A girl about their age, with short black hair and mischievous black eyes, stepped out from behind him.

"Hi."

Amos coughed. He nearly choked. Dunc pounded him on the back.

Uncle Woody laughed. "I call her Juan for short. Her given name is Juanita Carmen Avila Gonzalez. Juan seems easier." He turned to Juan. "Why don't you take the boys out and show them around before it gets dark, Juan-ita?"

"Sure. You guys come with me," she said. "I'll show you where we keep the horses."

She led them to the barn in back of the house. There were two horses in the corral.

24

One was white with dark spots on his rump, and the other was reddish brown.

"These are the horses we've picked out for you to ride while you're here. The sorrel is called Pete and the Appaloosa is Gomer."

Amos moved to the fence. He reached out and touched the sorrel.

Juan climbed up on the fence. "You can ride them if you want. Not very far, of course —it's almost dark. The tack is in the barn."

Amos looked at Dunc. "Tack? Why tacks? I thought you had to have a saddle and reins and stuff. Won't tacks hurt the horse?"

Juan smiled. "Maybe we'd better put off the riding until we have a chance to go over a couple of things."

Chapter·5

Amos thought he must be dreaming. No one in real life would be clanging on an iron bell at five o'clock in the morning. He rolled over and shut his eyes.

"Are you awake?" Dunc shook him.

Amos closed his eyes tighter.

Dunc shook him again. "Amos, didn't you hear the bell? I think it's time for breakfast."

"It's okay, Dunc. I'm dreaming, and you're a part of my dream. Go back to sleep."

"It's not a dream. Maria has breakfast ready. You have to get up."

Amos opened one eye. "Are you sure it's not a dream?"

Dunc nodded.

Amos slowly crawled down from the top bunk. "Why would they want to eat breakfast in the middle of the night?"

"It's early morning. Time to ride the range and do all that cowboy stuff, remember?"

"I remember. I just don't see what's wrong with doing it in the daylight."

Amos stumbled down the stairs behind Dunc. He followed him into the kitchen where Maria had stacks of pancakes waiting. Juan and Woody had already finished eating and were outside doing the chores.

Amos ate with one eye closed and his head propped up on Dunc's shoulder.

When they finished, Maria told them Juan was waiting for them out by the barn. They found her feeding the chickens. She let them help find the eggs, then showed them how to feed the horses and the milk cow.

When the chores were finished, Juan decided it was time for a riding lesson.

Amos was excited. He stepped up to Gomer and lifted his foot to the stirrup. The old horse moved. Not far, just a few inches. Amos stepped closer and lifted his foot again. The horse moved again. Every time Amos lifted his foot, Gomer moved.

Amos stepped around and looked the horse in the eye. "You don't by any chance know a dog named Scruff, do you?"

Gomer looked at him with big innocent brown eyes.

"No, I guess that's too long a shot."

Amos moved back to the stirrup and lifted his foot. Gomer craned his neck around and took a nibble out of Amos's shoulder.

"Aha!" Amos jumped back. "So you do know him."

Juan held Gomer's reins. "Now try it, Amos."

"You wimps having a hard time getting on your horsey? Maybe I could get you a ladder." An older boy had been watching them from the barn. He was laughing and pointing.

Juan put her hands on her hips. "Nice of you to show up, Billy Ray, now that all the chores are finished."

"You're not my boss, little girl. So quit acting like you are." The boy spat a wad of tobacco onto the ground and swaggered toward the house.

"Who was that?" Dunc asked.

Juan made a face. "That was a slimeball. His name is Billy Ray. He works here. Actually, he loafs here. The best way to handle him is to ignore everything he says or does."

"Why does my uncle put up with him?"

"He doesn't know how awful Billy Ray is. I haven't told him because I know how short-handed we are." Juan picked up the reins of Amos's horse. "Okay, let's try it again."

Amos climbed up on Gomer, and after a few lessons both boys were able to stop, go, and turn.

"You guys are doing great." Juan reached down and opened the gate. "Give your horses some rein and let them follow Molly, my mare. You'll be fine."

"Where are we going?" Amos asked.

"We're going to ride some of the ranch trails. Maria packed us a lunch so we can take our time. And while we're riding, we'll also be looking for El Diablo, your uncle's prize bull."

Amos stopped his horse. "Bull? As in big, with horns?"

Juan nodded.

Amos gulped. "I think I have something important to do in the house."

Dunc rode up beside him. "Come on, Amos. You wanted to be a real cowboy. Now's your chance."

Chapter · 6

The path narrowed, and the horses had to walk in single file. They were following a cattle trail up a canyon toward the mountains. Suzy, the collie, stayed ahead of the horses. She ran back every now and then and sat in the trail to make sure they were still coming.

"This would be a great place to shoot a western," Amos said. "I can just see the Indians swooping down from the rim of the canyon."

Juan turned in her saddle. "Actually, you're not too far off. This is Ghost Canyon. Legend has it that a battle did take place not too far from here."

She pointed up the canyon. "They say a

31

troop of cavalry soldiers carrying a shipment of gold ran into the Apaches and never made it out of this canyon. Some people think the soldiers' ghosts roam around up here protecting the gold."

"Maybe that's what those two guys on the plane are after," Dunc said.

Juan frowned. "What guys on what plane?"

Dunc told her the story, except for the part about Amos and the lady with the high heel.

"A lot of strange things have been happening around here," Juan said. "Maria's been getting these weird phone calls suggesting she should quit her job. Cattle are disappearing like flies. Banker Grimes has threatened to foreclose on the ranch. I've tried to talk to Woody about it, but he just tells me not to worry."

"That's what he told us," Amos said. "I think it's probably good advice."

Dunc and Juan both looked back at Amos. He ducked his head. "Okay. I can tell when I'm outnumbered."

Juan pulled her mare off the trail. "This is a good spot for lunch. Tie your horses real tight, or they won't be here when we get back."

Amos stepped off Gomer and, holding on to the reins, started for the nearest tree. But he couldn't move his right foot. Gomer was standing on the toe of his boot. Amos pushed and threatened, but Gomer just stood there, flattening Amos's toes and munching on grass without a care in the world.

Juan and Dunc had already tied their horses, grabbed the lunch bag, and were on the way up the hill to examine a nearby cave.

"Hey!" Amos yelled. "Somebody help me get this dumb animal off my foot! I'm starting to lose the feeling in my toes."

Juan turned around and cupped her hands. "He likes it if you talk nice to him."

"What?"

"Talk nice to him, and he'll move."

Amos glared at the horse. "You overweight mule, if my toes weren't starting to separate from my foot, I'd—" He took a deep breath. "Okay . . . nice horse. Good horse. Now, move your big fat foot."

Gomer didn't budge.

"You have to talk *really* nice!" Juan yelled down.

Amos turned red. He cleared his throat. "What a special, wonderful horse. I bet John

Wayne's horse wasn't half as good-looking as you are. You could probably be on television, you're such a good—"

Gomer picked up his foot and went on munching.

Amos limped over to a log and sat down. He pulled his boot off and massaged his aching toes. "Don't try that again, marshmallow lips, or you and I are going to have serious trouble."

Gomer snorted and blew snot all over him.

"Quit playing around down there, Amos!" Dunc yelled. "There's a neat cave up here with camping stuff and a bunch of boxes stored in it."

Amos finally climbed the steep hill and rejoined them. He stepped inside the cave. "Thank you both so much for your deep concern. I could have lost my toes down there. And I had horse-snot blown all over me. And Melissa—what about her?"

Dunc stared at him. "What does Melissa have to do with anything?"

"If my toes had been permanently damaged, I wouldn't be able to dance with her."

"Amos, you've never danced with Melissa.

She won't even talk to you. Or look at you. Or—"

"I'm confused," Juan interrupted. "Who's Melissa?"

"It's a long story," Dunc said. "I'll tell you about it some other time. Let's check out the crates under that tarp."

Amos lifted the corner of a dusty white tarp. "Look—there's something written on the sides of these boxes. I can't quite make it out."

Juan wiped the dust off. "It says 'Cookson Mining Company.' I'm going to open one. You guys help me find something I can use to pry the top off."

Amos stepped outside. He covered his eyes to protect them from the bright sunlight.

Suzy started barking furiously. She raced down the hill to the spot where they had tied their horses.

Amos focused. He looked down at the bottom of the canyon.

The horses were gone.

Chapter · 7

"It was the ghosts." Amos followed Dunc and Juan to the bottom of the canyon. "They probably let our horses loose so we'd be stuck up here and have to help them watch their gold —forever."

Dunc picked up a red bandanna. "Ghosts don't wear these."

"And they don't leave boot tracks either." Juan knelt down and traced a track in the dirt. "Somebody, a real person, deliberately let our horses go."

Dunc scratched his head. "Why would anybody want to do that to us?"

Juan stood up. "I don't know for sure. But

I'd be willing to bet it has something to do with those boxes up there in the cave."

"Well, I'm definitely not spending the night in this canyon with a bunch of ghosts." Amos started walking down the trail.

Juan grabbed his arm. "Hold on. You don't have to walk."

She put two fingers in her mouth and blew. A shrill whistle filled the air. In a few seconds they heard a whinny, and Molly came trotting up with Gomer and Pete close behind.

Juan rubbed Molly's forehead. "Isn't she special? I trained her from a foal. She knows to come if she hears me whistle, and usually the others follow."

"I'm glad," Dunc said. "I wasn't looking forward to walking back to the ranch. Before we start back, do you think we have enough time to check out those boxes?"

Juan grinned. "I was about to suggest it."

Dunc picked up a rock. "Let's open some boxes."

Amos looked around anxiously. "Did it ever occur to you two that whoever let our horses go could still be hiding around here somewhere?"

He was talking to air. Juan and Dunc had already scrambled up the hill.

Suzy stood by Amos and wagged her tail. He reached down and patted her head. "No one ever listens to me, Suzy. All I'm trying to say is—"

Suzy barked at him, then turned and ran up to the cave.

Amos held back a few minutes, shrugged, and followed her.

Dunc already had the lid off one box. "Mining equipment. Somebody's planning on doing some mining up here."

"Either that, or somebody thinks they know where some chests of gold are buried, and they're planning to dig them up," Juan said.

Amos shivered. "The ghost gold."

"That's my guess." Juan sat down. She took some sandwiches out of the lunch bag. "We'd better eat some of this food my grandmother packed, or she'll be upset."

Dunc took a sandwich. "We need to find out who this mining stuff belongs to. Whoever it is might be able to explain some of what's been going on around here."

Suzy started barking again.

A dark figure appeared in the mouth of the cave. The sunlight shone through his long hair and beard.

Amos moved closer to Dunc. "Tell me it's not a ghost. No—if it's a ghost, don't tell me until it's all over."

"I know who these things belong to." A bushy little man stepped forward out of the sun. "My name is Charlie Cookson. I work for the owner of these supplies—Woody Culpepper."

Chapter·8

Charlie Cookson explained that he was a mining engineer. He showed them a letter signed by Woody Culpepper authorizing him to take ore samples from the ranch for testing.

"It looks promising," Charlie said. "I've already sent off several samples. If they pan out, your uncle could be a very rich man."

Amos whistled. "Hey, that'd be great, Dunc! If my parents move away, maybe Uncle Woody will adopt me. Maybe buy me a new sports car so I could impress Melissa."

Dunc frowned. "Mr. Cookson, does anybody else know what you're doing up here?"

"My company, of course, and the young

man that works for your uncle. I think his name is Billy Ray. Why do you ask?"

"Some strange things have been happening around the ranch. If someone else was aware of what you were doing up here, it could answer a lot of questions."

"I hate to break this up," Juan said, "but if we don't start back now, we'll be riding in the dark."

Dunc stuck out his hand. "It's been nice talking with you, Mr. Cookson. If I'm ever up this way again, maybe we can visit some more."

"Anytime, young man. Oh, and tell your uncle I'm looking forward to meeting him in person."

They quietly rode out of the canyon until they reached the ranch road.

Amos broke the silence. "I don't get it. Why would your uncle Woody have mining equipment hidden in a cave and not tell anyone about it? He sure is going to a lot of trouble to keep everybody from finding out what he's doing."

Dunc frowned. "I don't get it either. Nothing makes sense. Charlie Cookson seemed like a nice guy. I don't think he was lying. But how does he tie in with everything else that's been going on? Uncle Woody wouldn't steal his own cows or make threatening calls to Maria."

"Woody obviously doesn't want us to know what's going on. Maybe he doesn't think he can trust any of us," Juan said.

Dunc shook his head. "I think there's more to all of this than we know."

It was almost dark when they rode up to the ranch house. They brushed and fed their horses and started for the house.

Amos had a hard time making his feet move. The ground seemed to sway under him. His legs bowed out, and his rear end was sore. Dunc thought about teasing him until he noticed that his own steps weren't very steady either.

"Well, I see the daisies made it back." Billy Ray stepped out of the shadows. "Did you wimps have a nice little walk?"

Juan moved up behind the boys. "What makes you think we had to walk anywhere, Billy Ray?"

Billy Ray coughed and stuttered. "I—I figured these city dudes would end up walking—that's all."

"Well, they didn't walk. Probably no thanks to you. In fact, they rode very well for their first time out."

"Who are you, Juan? Their mommy?" Billy Ray turned and melted back into the shadows.

"At least now we know it wasn't a ghost that let our horses go," Dunc said.

"No, it was a real-life sleazebag." Juan ran her fingers through her hair. "But why?"

"Maybe your uncle told him to, so we wouldn't find the mining supplies," Amos said.

"He wouldn't do that," Dunc said. "Billy Ray must have thought this one up on his own."

Juan laughed. "The only problem with that logic is Billy Ray doesn't have a brain."

Amos waddled toward the back door. "I'm going to do some serious soaking in a tub of hot water. As soon as possible."

Uncle Woody and Maria were waiting in the kitchen. Maria fussed over them and tried to get them to eat something.

Uncle Woody smiled. "We were about to come looking for you guys. I hope you didn't run into any trouble."

They looked at each other.

Dunc spoke first. "Not really. We were in Ghost Canyon looking for your prize bull, and we stopped to eat lunch in a cave up there." He watched his uncle's face. The expression didn't change.

Dunc went on. "Anyway, while we were eating lunch, our horses managed to get loose. Juan didn't have any trouble getting them back, though."

"Did you see any sign of the bull?"

"No," Juan answered. "We'll try again tomorrow."

"*We* may not be able to try again tomorrow," Amos groaned. "I'm not sure I can sit in a chair, much less ride a horse."

Uncle Woody smiled. "I really appreciate you boys helping out, but maybe tomorrow you should take it easy. Stay around here and help Maria."

Amos nodded gratefully. "Yeah, Maria probably needs someone to sample her doughnuts. I know it'll be a tough job—but what the heck—I volunteer."

"I'll race you to the tub," Dunc said.

"Right." Amos inched his way up the stairs. "It'll be the slowest race in history."

Chapter · 9

"You know, I think I may be getting the hang of this cowboy stuff." Amos popped another doughnut into his mouth.

"I don't think eating jelly doughnuts as fast as Maria can put them on the table is what your average cowboy does all day." Dunc brushed a crumb off his shirt and opened his notebook.

"What are you writing?" Amos asked.

"I'm making notes about the new evidence we uncovered yesterday about our case."

"I'm sorry I asked."

"Every good detective keeps a case notebook. When we become famous, these notes are going to be worth a lot of money."

"I don't think I'll hold my breath."

Dunc finished writing and slid the notebook into his shirt pocket. "If you're through stuffing doughnuts in your face, we need to do some investigating. Juan and Uncle Woody are off working on the windmill. And thanks to you, Maria's up to her elbows in flour. So now's the perfect time."

"I'd really like to play detective with you, Dunc, but I'm busy helping Maria. She told me she appreciates my appetite."

"I don't think that means she wants you to eat everything in sight."

"Okay, dudes, listen up." Billy Ray strutted through the kitchen door with his chest stuck out like a peacock's. "It's time to go to work. Culpepper left instructions for you to clean the barn."

"We saw him before he left this morning," Amos said. "He didn't mention anything to us about it."

"That's not my problem, chump. I'm only relaying the orders. You can find shovels and a pitchfork near the haystack. I'll come by later and check on your progress."

"If you think we're going to—"

"It's okay, Amos. Billy Ray's only doing his

job. We'd be happy to clean the barn. In fact, we'll get started on it right away." Dunc pulled Amos out the back door.

"Are you crazy?" Amos yelled.

"Keep your voice down."

"Keep my voice down? That guy is trying to get us to do his work!"

"I know."

"You know?"

Dunc nodded. "Billy Ray apparently wants us out of the way for a while. The question is, why?"

"What's the answer?"

"I don't know. But we're going to find out."

"Does this mean we're not going to clean the barn?"

"Not exactly."

Amos shook his head. "I don't get it. Are we cleaning the barn or aren't we?"

"One of us should stay here and work on the barn. In case Billy Ray comes out to check."

Amos's eyes narrowed. "Which one of us cleans the barn?"

"This could be a lucky break for us, Amos. I have a feeling about it."

"Me too. Which one of us cleans the barn?"

Dunc stopped. "Let's think about this thing logically. The one who stays should be the one who wants the experience of being a real cowboy. And the one who goes should be somebody who doesn't have a long—make that a very long—history of falling over things."

"Are you saying I'm clumsy?"

"Let's put it this way: A wrecking ball is an amateur compared to you."

Amos thought about it a second. "Okay. But you get back here as soon as you're through. I still have some serious food testing to do."

Chapter · 10

Dunc stayed in the shadows and worked his way back to the house. He inched up to the living-room window and peeked in. Billy Ray was talking in a low voice to someone over a shortwave radio.

"Right, boss. Everything's working the way you said it would. I'll meet you in fifteen minutes at the old adobe house."

Billy Ray hung up and came flying out the front door. Dunc barely made it around the corner of the house in time to avoid being caught.

Billy Ray went straight to his truck. He jumped in and took off before the truck door was completely shut. The tires sprayed gravel as he roared out of the driveway.

Dunc raced back to the barn. He found Amos shoveling manure out of a horse stall.

"Amos, something big is going on. I heard Billy Ray talking to someone on Uncle Woody's shortwave radio."

Amos dropped the shovel. "It's about time you got back. There are jelly doughnuts in that house with my name on them!"

"He's leaving now to meet with his accomplice and discuss their next move."

"So?"

"I heard Billy Ray say his part of the deal was in the bag."

"Dunc, this thing is getting away from you —big time."

"If we were to follow Billy Ray to his meeting, we might bust this thing wide open."

"I have a better idea. Let's go in the house, scarf down a few doughnuts, and wait for Juan and your uncle to get back. If they think it's important, they can call the sheriff."

Dunc shook his head. "We can't wait that long. Billy Ray already left."

"Hold it!"

"What?"

"Exactly how did you think we were going to follow him?"

"That's the tricky part."

Amos waited.

"We can't walk because he's driving, and he'd get too far ahead of us."

Amos waited.

"And neither one of us can drive. So I guess that means we'll have to ride. . . ."

Amos shook his head. "Forget it. There's no way you're going to get me on that horse again. I'm sore in places I didn't even know I had. I've decided my cowboy days are over. I'm going to spend the rest of my vacation helping Maria."

Dunc leaned back against the horse stall. "I understand, Amos. Really."

"You do?"

"Sure. If we were to crack this case, Melissa would probably go a little overboard with the hero worship. She might lose control completely. Who knows what would happen then?"

Amos thought about it. Not long. "Maybe I could put a pillow in the saddle. . . ."

Dunc smiled and headed for the corral.

Chapter · 11

Saddling the horses took longer than Dunc had planned. Gomer ran around the corral until Amos assured him he was the best-looking and most intelligent horse on the ranch, probably on the planet.

Even after the saddles were on, things didn't go too well. Dunc's saddle turned sideways every time he stepped in the stirrup, and Amos put his saddle on facing the wrong direction.

After about an hour and several more tries, they managed to saddle and bridle both horses. Before they left, Dunc pinned a note on the barn wall telling his uncle where they would be.

Billy Ray's tire tracks were easy to follow. They stayed on the main road for a few miles, then turned south up a canyon bed.

Amos stood in the stirrups to avoid sitting. After a few miles he pulled his horse to a stop and stepped down. "I've changed my mind. Not even Melissa is worth this much pain."

Dunc stopped. "Just think, Amos. When they talk about this in the future—and they will—your name will be right up there with all the famous cowboys like Wyatt Earp, Pat Garrett—"

"Calamity Jane. I don't know if I can stand this much longer, Dunc. We're talking major pain here."

"Listen—do you hear anything?"

"Only the sound of my poor body begging me to go home and soak in a hot tub."

"Cows. I hear cows—lots of them!"

Amos closed his eyes. "I hate to break it to you, but this is a ranch. There are supposed to be cows on it."

Dunc rode around the next bend. "Not this many in one place. Come up here and have a look."

About a hundred head of cattle were contained in a makeshift barbed-wire corral.

Billy Ray's old truck was parked in front of a falling-down adobe house, along with a brand-new black and silver pickup with dark tinted windows.

Dunc stepped off. "We'll tie our horses over there behind that boulder. We need to get closer. If we keep low and move through the cows, I don't think they'll spot us."

Amos looked at the cattle. One of them stood out. He was twice the size of the others. He snorted and pawed the ground. "Dunc, do you remember that bull your uncle lost? I think we've found him."

"El Diablo?" Dunc swallowed. "I wouldn't worry about him. He's probably just your basic harmless bull. We'll try and work around him." Dunc started toward the cows. "Are you coming?"

Amos was about to tell him how stupid the whole idea was—when he heard a rattling sound at his feet.

"Snake!"

Amos plowed over the top of Dunc, burying him facedown in the sand. He hurdled the corral fence and landed on his knees. He looked up—straight into a pair of big, ugly, bloodred eyes.

El Diablo snorted, and steam came out of both nostrils. He lowered his head and pointed his long horns in Amos's direction. Amos rolled under the fence just as the bull charged.

Dunc was waiting on the other side. "Amos, you were supposed to work around him. Now you have him mad!"

Amos opened his mouth to tell Dunc exactly what he thought about him and the bull, when he felt himself being lifted off the ground.

Billy Ray and a man who was roughly the size of a house stood over them. The giant had Amos by the collar.

Billy Ray grinned. "Boys, meet Bubba."

Amos tried to get his feet to touch the ground. "Nice to meet you, Mr. Bubba—sir. Actually, we were just leaving."

Billy Ray sneered. "Not hardly. Bring them along, Bubba. The boss will know what to do with them."

Bubba grabbed Dunc with his free hand and easily carried them both into the house.

A heavyset man wearing an expensive black suit was seated at a table studying a map. He stood up when he saw the boys. "What's going on?"

"We found us some snoopers, Mr. Grimes." Billy Ray spat a wad of tobacco onto the floor. "Do you want Bubba to squash 'em?"

Dunc dangled from Bubba's hand. "Are you J. B. Grimes? The bank president?"

"Billy Ray, you idiot! Now they've seen me. They can tie me in with all this."

"I'm sorry, Mr. Grimes. I guess I didn't think of that."

"That's your problem, Billy Ray—you don't think. Mr. Cookson will be here shortly, and if he sees them, everything will be ruined."

"You want Bubba to squash 'em?"

"Don't be moronic. Lock them in the old outhouse until Cookson leaves. Then we'll decide what to do with them."

Bubba carried them outside. He opened the door of an old dilapidated outhouse and pushed them in.

"What are you going to do with us?" Amos asked.

Billy Ray picked his teeth. "Bubba likes to squash people, so don't do nothing stupid. Keep your mouths shut until after Mr.

Grimes's guest leaves." He shut the door and barred it from the outside.

Amos sat down on the wooden bench trying to avoid the hole in the middle. "It smells in here. Bad."

Dunc sat on the other side. "I know, Amos. I'm working on a way out."

"Maybe we ought to stay."

"What?"

"Bubba squashes people."

"Billy Ray only said that to scare us."

"It worked."

Dunc tapped his chin. "Do you remember when my grandpa Culpepper came to visit us? I think we were about six."

"I think the smell in here is affecting your brain."

"It was Halloween, and he was telling us what kids used to do for fun on Halloween when he was young. Do you remember?"

Amos sighed. "I'm positive you're going to tell me."

"They pushed over outhouses."

"You're not thinking of—"

"Why not? If we start rocking it from side to side, it's bound to fall over."

Amos stood up. "When your grandfather

and his friends pushed over those outhouses —were they empty?"

"I suppose."

"This one isn't!"

"I know that, Amos. But if we do it right, it'll fall gently over on its side, and nobody will get hurt, and we'll be free. It's worth a try. Besides, who knows what Bubba will do to us after Grimes finishes his business with Mr. Cookson?"

"I guess you have a point."

"Okay. We'll push on my side first and try to get it rocking back and forth. . . . Ready? Go."

The rickety outhouse groaned and shuddered on the first push. By the third push, they had it rocking.

"Get ready, Amos. It's going ov—"

Dunc slid into Amos, and the outhouse fell over with a loud crash. The walls were so old, they collapsed on top of the boys.

Amos lay flat on his back covered with pieces of the outhouse. He could feel something warm licking his face. He opened his eyes. It was Suzy, making sure he was still alive.

Chapter · 12

Amos blinked and sat up. Dunc groaned next to him and rolled into a sitting position. Amos pushed a last board away and found himself looking up at Uncle Woody.

"What are you doing here?" Amos asked.

Uncle Woody patted the boys on the back and helped them up. "You boys really saved the day. It's a good thing Juan found your note telling us where you were, or we might not have been able to get the sheriff here in time. Grimes was ready to ship the cattle out."

Nearby, the deputies were escorting Banker Grimes to the patrol car. Billy Ray and Bubba were taking turns telling the sheriff everything they had done wrong since they were born. It took a while, but they eventually got around to this particular crime.

Grimes had hired them to help put Uncle Woody out of business by stealing his cows, convincing his help to quit, and reporting every move he made.

Grimes had stumbled onto a preliminary report prepared years ago by a small mining company suggesting the strong possibility of a uranium strike on the ranch, near Ghost Canyon. To investigate it, he had hired Charlie Cookson over the phone, pretending to be the owner of the ranch, Woody Culpepper.

Dunc beamed. "We're glad we could help." He looked at Amos. "Right, Amos?"

Amos glared at him.

Dunc elbowed him. "*Right,* Amos?"

"I guess so."

Charlie Cookson walked over and shook hands with Uncle Woody. "I'd like to apologize, Mr. Culpepper. I had no idea I wasn't dealing with you. I should have been suspicious, I suppose, but a lot of my clients demand strict confidentiality, so it didn't seem all that unusual."

"It worked out okay," Woody said. "Tell me, just how big is this strike, anyway?"

"It's big. Maybe even the biggest in history. You could be a very rich man, Mr. Culpepper."

The word *rich* caught Amos's ear. He moved closer to Uncle Woody. "You don't have any children, do you?"

"Amos." Dunc elbowed him again.

"I only wanted to let him know I'm available."

"That's great, Amos." Uncle Woody smiled. "I'll keep you in mind."

Juan rode up, leading their horses. "Sure, Amos, you could come out here to live. That way you could ride old Gomer every day."

Amos spun around and started walking toward the truck. "On second thought," he yelled over his shoulder, "my parents would probably be heartbroken. I know my sister would miss me terribly. And my dog—well, he loves me so much."

Dunc grinned and started after him. "And the moon is made of green cheese, Santa Claus is real, Elvis is alive. . . ."

**Be sure to join Dunc and Amos in these
other Culpepper Adventures:**

The Case of the Dirty Bird

When Dunc Culpepper and his best friend, Amos,
first see the parrot in a pet store, they're not impressed—it's smelly, scruffy, and missing half its
feathers. They're only slightly impressed when
they learn that the parrot speaks four languages,
has outlived ten of its owners, and is probably 150
years old. But when the bird starts mouthing off
about buried treasure, Dunc and Amos get pretty
excited—let the amateur sleuthing begin!

Dunc's Doll

Dunc and his accident-prone friend, Amos, are up
to their old sleuthing habits once again. This time
they're after a band of doll thieves! When a doll
that once belonged to Charles Dickens's daughter
is stolen from an exhibition at the local mall, the
two boys put on their detective gear and do some
serious snooping. Will a vicious watchdog keep
them from retrieving the valuable missing doll?

Culpepper's Cannon

Dunc and Amos are researching the Civil War cannon that stands in the town square when they find a note inside telling them about a time portal. Entering it through the dressing room of La Petite, a women's clothing store, the boys find themselves in downtown Chatham on March 8, 1862—the day before the historic clash between the *Monitor* and the *Merrimac*. But the Confederate soldiers they meet mistake them for Yankee spies. Will they make it back to the future in one piece?

Dunc Gets Tweaked

Dunc and Amos meet up with a new buddy named Lash when they enter the radical world of skateboard competition. When somebody "cops"—steals—Lash's prototype skateboard, the boys are determined to get it back. After all, Lash is about to shoot for a totally rad world's record! Along the way they learn a major lesson: *Never* kiss a monkey!

Dunc's Halloween

Dunc and Amos are planning the best route to get the most candy on Halloween. But their plans change when Amos is slightly bitten by a were-

wolf. He begins scratching himself and chasing
UPS trucks—he's become a werepuppy!

Dunc Breaks the Record

Dunc and Amos have a small problem when they
try hang gliding—they crash in the wilderness.
Luckily, Amos has read a book about a boy who
survived in the wilderness for fifty-four days. Too
bad Amos doesn't have a hatchet. Things go from
bad to worse when a wild man holds the boys cap-
tive. Can anything save them now?

Dunc and the Flaming Ghost

Dunc's not afraid of ghosts, although Amos is sure
that the old Rambridge house is haunted by the
ghost of Blackbeard the Pirate. Then the best
friends meet Eddie, a meek man who claims to be
impersonating Blackbeard's ghost in order to live
in the house in peace. But if that's true, why are
flames shooting from his mouth?

Amos Gets Famous

Deciphering a code they find in a library book,
Amos and Dunc stumble onto a burglary ring. The
burglars' next target is the home of Melissa, the
girl of Amos's dreams (who doesn't even know
that he's alive). Amos longs to be a hero to Me-

lissa, so nothing will stop him from solving this case—not even a mind-boggling collision with a jock, a chimpanzee, and a toilet.

Dunc and Amos Hit the Big Top

In order to impress Melissa, Amos decides to perform on the trapeze at the visiting circus. Look out below! But before Dunc can talk him out of his plan, the two stumble across a mystery behind the scenes at the circus. Now Amos is in double trouble. What's really going on under the big top?

Dunc's Dump

Camouflaged as piles of rotting trash, Dunc and Amos are sneaking around the town dump. Dunc wants to find out who is polluting the garbage at the dump with hazardous and toxic waste. Amos just wants to impress Melissa. Can either of them succeed?

Dunc and the Scam Artists

Dunc and Amos are at it again. Some older residents of their town have been bilked by con artists, and the two boys want to look into these crimes. They meet elderly Betsy Dell, whose nasty nephew Frank gives the boys the creeps. Then they notice some soft dirt in Ms. Dell's shed, and a shovel. Does Frank have something horrible in store for Dunc and Amos?

Dunc and Amos and the Red Tattoos

Dunc and Amos head for camp and face two weeks of fresh air—along with regulations, demerits, KP, and inedible food. But where these two best friends go, trouble follows. They overhear a threat against the camp director and discover that camp funds have been stolen. Do these crimes have anything to do with the tattoo of the exotic red flower that some of the camp staff have on their arms?

Dunc's Undercover Christmas

It's Christmastime! Dunc, Amos, and Amos's cousin T.J. hit the mall for some serious shopping. But when the seasonal magic is threatened by some disappearing presents and Santa Claus himself is a prime suspect, the boys put their celebration on hold and go undercover in the perfect Christmas disguises! Can the sleuthing trio protect Santa's threatened reputation and catch the impostor before he strikes again?

The Wild Culpepper Cruise

When Amos wins a "Why I Love My Dog" contest, he and Dunc are off on the Caribbean cruise of their dreams! But there's something downright fishy about Amos's suitcase and before they know it, the two best friends wind up with more high seas adventure than they bargained for. Can Dunc and Amos figure out who's out to get them and salvage what's left of their vacation?

Dunc and the Haunted Castle

When Dunc and Amos are invited to spend a week in Scotland, Dunc can already hear the bagpipes a-blowin'. But when the boys spend their first night in an ancient castle, it isn't bagpipes they hear. It's moans! Dunc hears groaning coming from inside his bedroom walls. Amos notices the eyes of a painting following him across the room! Could the castle really be haunted? Local legend has it that the castle's former lord wanders the ramparts at night in search of his head! Team up with Dunc and Amos as they go ghostbusting in the Scottish Highlands!